Illustrations: Ann de Bode
Original title: *Opa duurt ontelbaar lang*
© Van In, Lier, 1995. Van In Publishers, Grote Markt 39,
2500 Lier, Belgium.
© in this edition Evans Brothers Limited 1997
(world English rights excluding the USA and Canada)
English text by Su Swallow

First published in Great Britain by
Evans Brothers Limited
2A Portman Mansions
Chiltern Street
London W1M 1LE

Printed by KHL (Singapore)

0 237 51755 8

British Library Cataloguing in Publication data.
A catalogue record for this book is available from the
British Library.

HELPING HANDS

GRANDAD, I'LL ALWAYS REMEMBER YOU

ANN DE BODE AND RIEN BROERE

Evans Brothers Limited

Tom is in a hurry to get home.
School has finished early,
and he's got lots of plans for the afternoon.
He might build a den, or play football.
Or he might go on his bike.
He's in such a good mood he even starts to sing.

He looks in through the window.
What's this? The house is full of people.
Mum is there, and his sister Kate.
Uncle John and Aunt Lucy are there too.
And he can see Grandma.
Tom bursts in.
'Hallo,' he calls. 'It's me!'
Nobody says a word.

Something is going on, Tom thinks.
He looks round the room.
All these people together.
That usually means there is a party.
But nobody looks very happy today.
They are staring into space, and sighing.
All of a sudden, Tom stops feeling cheerful.
An odd feeling wells up inside him.

Mum comes over to him.
She kneels down and hugs him.
Tom looks at her. Her eyes are red, and
there's a black smudge on her cheek.
'Tom,' she says. 'Something very sad has happened.'
'Yes,' says Tom.
He doesn't know what else to say.
'Grandad...' Mum says quietly, 'Grandad has died.'

'Oh dear!' says Grandma. 'Oh dear, oh dear!'
Tom looks at her. He wants to give her a kiss.
He wants to make her smile, but doesn't know how.
'Grandad is dead,' he says simply.
'Yes,' says Grandma. 'Your grandad is dead.'
'For ever?' asks Tom.
'Yes,' says Grandma. 'When you die, it's for ever.'
For ever, thinks Tom. That's a very, very long time.

'The day started the same as usual,' says Grandma.
She shakes her head. She remembers everything.
'Grandad got up first, and made breakfast.
Then he gave me a big hug.
But after breakfast he stood up and said,
"I feel very tired." I told him to go and lie down
while I cleared the table.
"You're an angel," Grandad said.'

'A bit later, I had an odd feeling,' Grandma continues.
'I knew something was wrong.
I went over to the settee. Grandad was lying there,
very quiet, very still, very peaceful.
And I knew that he was dead.
I wasn't afraid. I just thought, it can't be true.
I gave him a last big kiss.
And then I cried. I cried and cried.'

Kate comes over to sit next to Tom.
He can see she wants to tell him something.
'Tom,' she says, 'it's as though Grandad's battery
ran down and stopped.'
'But Grandad wasn't an alarm clock!' cries Tom.
'I'm just trying to explain that when you die,
everything stops.'
'Well I don't like stories that end like that,' says Tom.

Dad comes in. He's home earlier than usual.
He looks pale and upset.
'Oh Martin,' Mum says to Dad.
She puts her arms around him and starts crying.
They hold each other very tight.
They don't want to let each other go.
Tom looks at his mum and dad.
He's never seen them so upset.

A stranger arrives.
He looks very serious, and shakes everyone's hand.
Even Tom's.
And he says something Tom doesn't understand.
'This man has come to help us,' says Mum.
'When someone dies, there's a lot to do.'
'What will happen to Grandad now?' asks Tom.
It's his grandad, so he wants to know everything.

'When you're dead,' says Mum,
'you're put in a wooden coffin,
which has soft pillows in it.
Then the coffin is put into a grave in the ground.
Or it is burnt and the ashes are put in an urn.'
'Won't Grandad be afraid?' asks Tom.
'No,' says Mum. 'When you're dead,
you don't feel anything any more.'

The man has taken some books out of his case.
He starts looking through them with Grandma.
'Would you like to come and help me?' asks Grandma.
'We have to choose some flowers.'
Grandma takes Tom on to her lap.
The book is full of flowers in soft colours.
'We must choose the most beautiful ones,' says Tom.
'The best flowers for the best grandad in the world.'

Mum tells Tom what is happening.
'Grandad is lying in his coffin.
But the coffin isn't closed yet,
and we can go to see him one last time.'
'I want to go too,' says Tom.
'But isn't it a bit frightening?'
'It's sad, but not frightening,' says Mum.
'It's as if Grandad was fast asleep.'

'When Grandad is buried, a car
will take the coffin to the church,' says Mum.
'Will Grandad be put in a big car like that?' asks Tom,
looking at a picture in the man's book.
'Yes,' says Mum.
That's good, Tom thinks.
Grandad deserves a big car
because he was someone special.

'Mum, where do you go when you're dead?' asks Tom.
'Well, it's hard to explain.
You see, Grandad has died, so
he's not there any more.
But as long as we keep thinking about him,
he will still be with us in a way.
And you won't forget him, will you?'
'Never!' says Tom. 'He will be in my heart for ever.'

Tom remembers how Grandad used to spoil him.
With sweets and ices and lots of other things.
And Grandad could always answer his questions.
'Mum,' says Tom suddenly. 'Does Grandad know he's dead?'
'Well, no, I don't think so,' she says. 'When you're dead,
you don't know about anything any more.
So you don't know you're dead.
But stop worrying about it. Go out and play.'

Stop worrying about it?
That's easier said than done, thinks Tom.
Grandad used to know everything,
and now he doesn't know he's dead!
And I can't tell him, because he's not there any more.
It must be hard, not knowing you're dead.
I must tell him! But how?

'You look very sad, Tom,' says a neighbour.
'I'm looking for Grandad, to tell him
something,' says Tom.
'And you don't know where he is?'
'Nobody knows,' says Tom. 'He's died.'
'Oh dear!' says the neighbour.
'Your grandad has passed away?'
'No, he's not passed anything. He's dead,' replies Tom.

The neighbour comes to sit beside Tom.
'Lots of people are afraid of death,' she says.
'That's why they sometimes use different words,
like "passed away", or "gone up to the clouds".'
They both look up.
No grandad there.
'No,' says Tom. 'He's not there.'
So how can he help his grandad?

21

Tom thinks about what the neighbour said.
Grandad has gone up to the clouds.
Maybe there's a town called 'The Clouds'.
In that case, thinks Tom, I can do something.
I can call Grandad.
He opens a drawer and pulls out the phone book.

Dad can see what Tom wants to do.
'Tom, you can't ring Grandad, you know.
What you can do is to think about him very hard.
If you like, I'll ask Grandma to give you
Grandad's goldfish.
You can look after them, and
every time you look at them,
you'll think of Grandad.'

Tom can't get to sleep.
He tosses and turns, and thinks about Grandad.
Being dead is very serious, he thinks.
He tries to imagine what it's like to be dead.
He tries to lie quite still, but he can't.
When you're alive you can't pretend to be dead.
Then he thinks about Grandad's goldfish.
That cheers him up a bit.

Tom gives a big sigh.
He turns on his side.
Now he can look at Grandad.
He's put his picture on the bedside table.
The night light shines on it.
Grandad is smiling at him.
Grandad doesn't know he's dead, thinks
Tom, otherwise he wouldn't look so happy.

Suddenly Tom has an idea.
He could write a letter
and put it into the coffin
when they go to see Grandad for the last time.
Maybe that way the letter will get
to where Grandad is now.
And if he reads the letter, he'll know.
Tom is pleased with his plan.

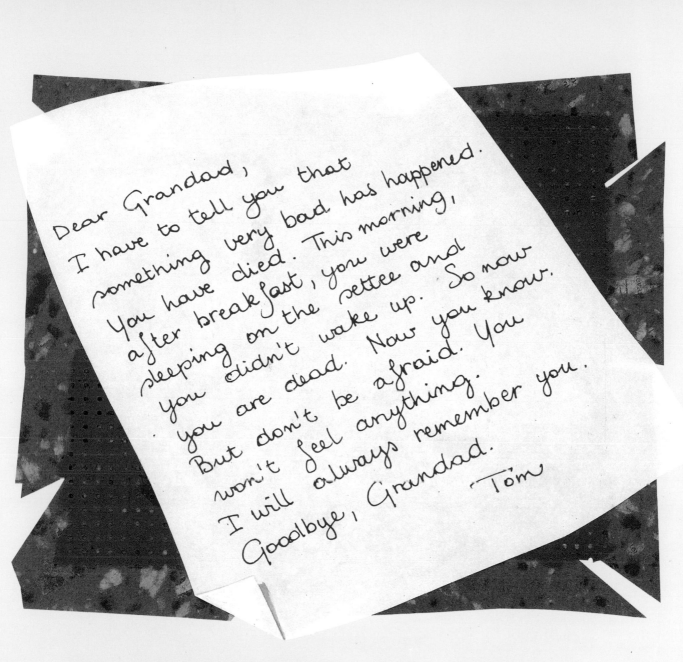

Dear Grandad, he writes.
I have to tell you that something
very bad has happened.
You have died. This morning, after breakfast,
you were sleeping on the settee and you didn't
wake up. So now you are dead. Now you know.
But don't be afraid. You won't feel anything.
I will always remember you. Goodbye, Grandad.

Tom is dreaming. In his dream,
he is watching a goldfish swimming in a bowl.
The fish turns and swims towards Tom.
Its face turns into Grandad's face.
'Tom, Tom,' mouths the fish.
The glass reflects Tom's smiling face.
Grandad seems to swim right through it.

The dream isn't over yet.
Tom hears a tapping on the window.
It's Grandad!
In his sleep, Tom gets up and opens the window.
'Hallo, Tom,' says Grandad.
Tom starts to speak, but it's too late.
Grandad is moving away, getting fainter and fainter.

Tom snatches up the letter.
'Grandad, wait! I've got a letter for you.'
But Grandad has almost disappeared.
Tom holds the letter out of the window.
He feels it being pulled out of his hand.
Then he wakes up with a start.
Dad has his arm round Tom.

'You've been sleepwalking,' says Dad.
'You even opened the window in your sleep.'
Tom feels very confused.
'I saw Grandad,' he says.
'No Tom,' Dad says gently. 'You've been dreaming.'
'I really saw him,' says Tom. 'He was here.'
'Shhh now,' whispers Dad.
'Try to go back to sleep.'

When Dad has gone, Tom turns on his bedside lamp.
He looks at Grandad's picture again.
And then he realises - the letter has gone!
So I wasn't dreaming after all, thinks Tom.
Good. Now Grandad will be able to read it.
With a sigh of relief he snuggles down
and falls fast asleep.

Outside, the wind is blowing.
A white piece of paper is carried up by the wind.
It floats up into the dark night.
Higher and higher it goes,
until all you can see is a small white dot.
Just like a bird flying to its nest.